READY, STEADY, RACE!

For Ready Steady Eddie, Toot-Toot Tom,
Rickshaw Rafi and Go-Kart Gabe –
on your marks, get set, RACE! x

S.P-H.

For Theodore,
my little apprentice!

E.E.

HODDER CHILDREN'S BOOKS

First published in Great Britain in 2019 by Hodder and Stoughton

1 3 5 7 9 10 8 6 4 2

Text copyright © Smriti Prasadam-Halls 2019
Illustration copyright © Ed Eaves 2019

The moral rights of the author and illustrator have been asserted.

HB ISBN: 978 1 444 93313 0
PB ISBN: 978 1 444 93314 7

Printed in China

FSC
www.fsc.org

MIX
Paper from
responsible sources
FSC® C104740

Hodder Children's Books
An imprint of
Hachette Children's Group
Part of Hodder and Stoughton
Carmelite House
50 Victoria Embankment
London, EC4Y 0DZ

An Hachette UK Company
www.hachette.co.uk

www.hachettechildrens.co.uk

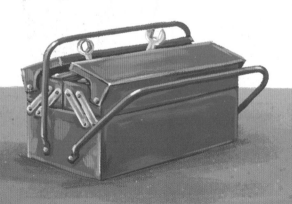

Ready, Steady, RACE!

Smriti Prasadam-Halls & Ed Eaves

Welcome, welcome, champion racers,
MIGHTY motors,
SPEEDY chasers.

Here's the track to test your skill,
Stay the course and feel the thrill!
Ignitions on and turbos **WHIRRING**,
Pistons pumping, engines purring.

Who is going to take first place?
Ready, steady... **RACE! RACE! RACE!**

RACE CAR RANI takes the lead,
Burning rubber
with her speed.

VROOM, **VROOM, VROOMING,**
ZOOM, ZOOM, ZOOMING!

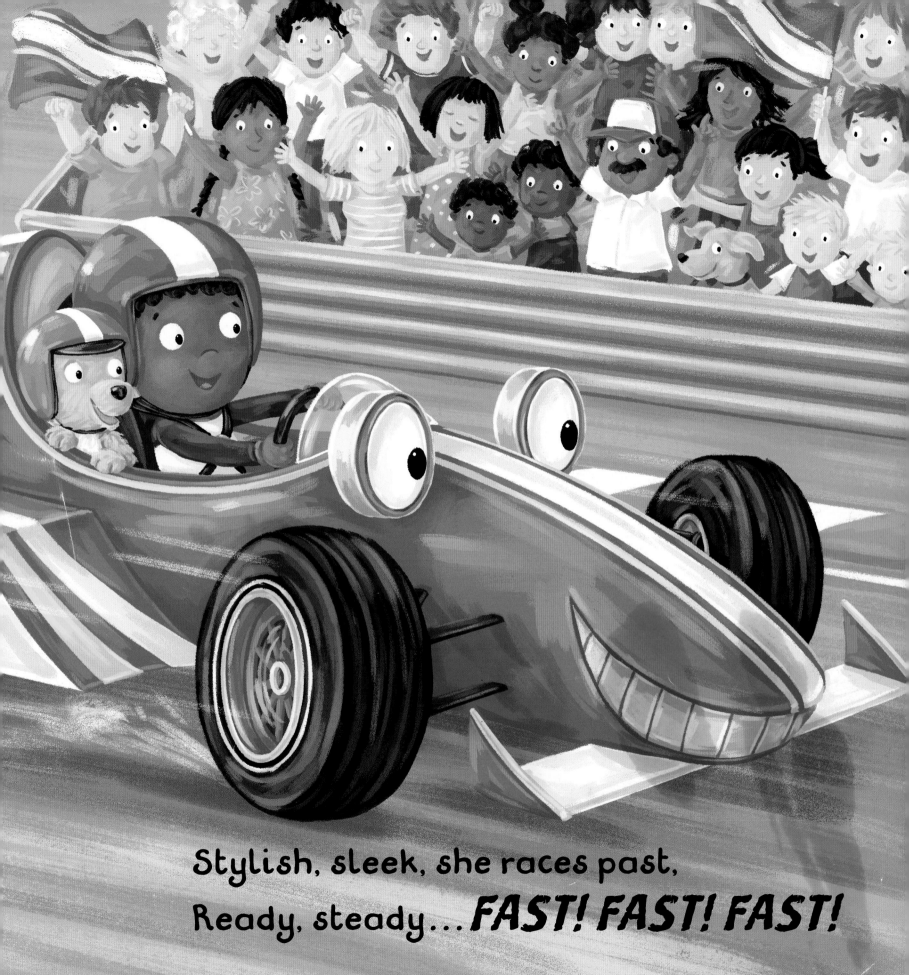

Stylish, sleek, she races past,
Ready, steady . . . **FAST! FAST! FAST!**

Here comes speedy **JONAS JET**,
He's the fastest racer yet!

SWOOPING,

SOARING,

engine roaring,

Gaining speed
up in the sky,
Ready, steady...

FLY, FLY, FLY!

TRINI TRAIN

is right on track,
She hurtles on, not looking back.

CHUGGING, PEEPING, WHISTLING, SCREECHING,

Swift and smooth,
she's racing through,
Ready, steady...
CHOO, CHOO, CHOO!

The track's all bumpy, wet and steep,
Now first in line zooms **JOSHI JEEP.**

SLISHING,
SLOSHING,

SQUELCHING, SQUASHING,

He has tyres that never slip,
Ready, steady... **GRIP! GRIP! GRIP!**

SPEEDBOAT SAM gives one big swoosh,
And cuts the water with a whoosh!

SKIMMING,

SLIDING,

CHOPPING,

GLIDING,

With a splash he speeds away,
Ready, steady...

But now a super speedy stunt,
Puts **MOTORBIKE MIKE** way out in front.

Zig-zag **CURVING,**

turning, SWERVING,

The fastest motorbike there is,
Ready, steady... WHIZZ! WHIZZ! WHIZZ!

But suddenly his motor's choking,
The engine's hot and now it's **SMOKING!**

JUD-JUD-**JUDDERING,**
GASPING,
SPLUTTERING,

He'll **NEVER**
win the contest now,
He's sure he'll have to stop, but...

...**WOW!**

The other racers start to brake,

No one tries to overtake.

The racers want to HELP their friend,

So he can make it to the end.

GO MIKE!

Come on, Mike, just hang on in!